AF066888

The Silk Road To Samarkand

Derf Nögard

Copyright © 2021 by Derf Nögard

All rights reserved. No part of this book may be reproduced or used in any manner without written permission of the copyright owner except for the use of quotations in a book review.

ISBNs:
Paperback: 978-1-80227-129-4
eBook: 978-1-80227-130-0

Contents

Chapter One 1

Chapter Two 9

Chapter Three. 15

Chapter Four. 25

Chapter Five 39

Chapter Six 41

Chapter Seven 47

Chapter Eight 49

Chapter Nine 57

Chapter Ten 65

Chapter Eleven 69

Chapter Twelve 75

Chapter Thirteen 79

Chapter Fourteen 89

Chapter One

'Hello, Fred. How are you doing, dear boy?' Grandfather's jovial booming voice enveloped me like the aroma of an expensive French meal, a lovely promise of goodies to come.

'I'm fine, Grandfather. I've sorted where they are and how we get there. Isfahan is in Persia, or Iran as it is now called; Samarkand is in Uzbekistan. They are approximately 900 to 1000 miles apart. I know Nettie wants to do it on a camel, but the train would be far more suitable. What shall I suggest to her? My feelings are a bit of both, arriving at Samarkand on a camel. What do you think?'

'Nettie makes sweeping proclamations, but she's never been on the back of a camel. They wiggle as they walk and make you fearfully seasick. She needs a steady ride, smooth and comfortable, propped up by cushions. I suggest some train travel, a motor vehicle and about three steps on a camel; four at the very most. Getting her up on its back will be a feat. The availability of a crane will not be an option, I fear. We need a collapsible ladder.'

'But the camel sits down; you don't have to climb up.'

'With Nettie, you assume nothing. I agree that the camel should be the final means at the gates of Samarkand.'

'With faithful Rashid leading her in triumph through the great gates into the Reqistan Piazza.'

'Then back by the deluxe train in our own suite with luxury bathroom, all the way to Tehran, and on by British Airways. Genuinely no money left. She can then go back to her reserved spot on the English Jurassic Coast, and be found by the British Museum, and strung on wires on display forever.'

'I shall miss her, Grandfather, I really will. Going for a visit to the British Museum can never give the same excitement as when she is alive. She can scare you witless, and terrify the spines of your back, but you still want her to be in your life, alive and giving instructions, making you jump through hoops.'

'You're becoming very wise for your age, but you're not turning green like you should. We all set off pink, then turn green, like some of those

Chapter One

plants that produce red leaves that turn green. Pieris Forrestii is one I remember. It starts at the tip of your ears, then goes right through you. The dye ran out before it could get to the tip of my tail, and nothing has budged any further. One green dragon, one pink tip of a tail.'

'Will I be like that?'

'No idea. You might and you might not. Wait and see.'

'It's a useful thing, like a valve. It tells you if you're happy, or if you're cross, and what rate of happy or cross so you can then decide what to do. Useful as a light on a dark night, switch it on or off. Green tail tips are boring. Pink helps you to enjoy life. Ah well, let's go see Nettie and have a good natter about our journey.' So, we set off gleefully for Aunt Nettie's house to find her looking through old copies of Vogue.

'Hello, boys. Nice to see you. Are you both well and happy or has this dull weather defeated you?'

'We're both fine, Nettie, and you?'

'Bones a bit creaky but then they're well past their sell-by date.' She turned a few pages of her magazine with a despairing look on her face.

Chapter One

'What has happened to clothes nowadays? It's all like tramps, no hems, uneven edges, slashes in trousers and sleeves, fastenings with sticky tape, undergarments on view for all to see. No good colours. All out of the rag bag, thrown on anything; have no pride in yourself. Live in a dirty shop doorway and beg for money to buy drugs. This new century is a mess. I want to go back to the days of beautiful silk, exquisitely made into perfectly fitting creations that enhance the wearer, not reduce them to the lowest levels.'

'Not a good start, Grandfather.'

'She might be persuaded to take a suite on the train, in that case. What do you think?'

'Let's try it. Nettie, Fred here wanted to know if you would take the train from Isfahan to Samarkand, it being about a thousand miles. Long way on a camel. Luxury train; all meals provided; bathroom built in. What do you think?'

'I think that the train didn't exist at the time I wanted to go, back in the days of the Shah.'

Grandfather shook his head - a very decisive shake, not a what-shall-we-do shake, and turned to Nettie.

'Put down your magazines and listen. Fred here has done a thorough job. Looked at all the books he can find and immersed himself in the countries concerned: Uzbekistan, Turkmenistan, Iran, even parts of Russia. He's studied climate and found that April and October are the best months. Any other time is either too hot or too cold!'

'We fly to Tehran by British Airways overnight and go by 4x4 vehicle to Isfahan, perhaps even further. Then we join the train or another vehicle to the next stop, Samarkand, then by camel actually into the city. Then board the Golden Eagle on its last journey of the year at the end of October.'

Nettie closed her eyes tight shut, as she does at the start of Dragon's Drive. She was clearly sorting out the details. Her mouth moved as though she was speaking, but not a sound emerged. This went on for at least ten minutes, then she opened her eyelids and looked directly at her visitors.

'Yes, boys, that sounds a well-considered journey. It can snow from the end of October and we don't want that. You've done a good job, Fred. A very good job…. all that is left is the timing of the start so we don't miss the last Eagle.' Grandfather beamed – a very happy dragon.

Chapter One

'Yes, Fred, you make an excellent travel agent. Heathrow to Tehran timetable required. The Golden Eagle starts in Almaty in Kazakhstan and gets to Tehran in 17 days and 15 nights. We join at Samarkand 5 days into the journey. I pulled out my timetable and showed them the route. Big countries very varied geography.'

'Yes, Fred. It's only when you leave England that you realise how small a country it is. Everyone else seems vastly bigger.'

'Thank you for all you've done, I look forward to the detailed itinerary in due course.' Aunt Nettie saw us off, clearly pleased, and we went away utterly delighted that we'd managed an agreement so quickly.

'So, it's a matter of finding out exact distances and modes of transport. Then, pulling everything together to arrive at the dates of departure, and booking the Golden Eagle.'

'All organised and, hopefully, no disasters or pickles.'

I looked up at the larger dragon with true affection. I liked Grandfather to get into pickles; it livened life up.

Chapter Two

Grandfather and I arrived at Nettie's door on the dot, both together, I with my official clipboard with all the times of departures and arrivals, all modes of transport, all confirmations and deposits paid. I felt proud to have managed it, and I had a copy in my suitcase on DVD.

Gladys answered the bell. 'Good morning, Master Fred. She's ready, just putting a final touch to the wrappings around the cheese sandwiches.'

'Oh no! Not cheese sandwiches again…'

'There'll be a time when you'll be glad of my forethought. Good morning, Fred and Chauncey. Nice day for a flight to Persia. No rain there, but then, there never is.' I just dare not ask if she packed her Sunday supplements, but felt sure she will have done.

'Morning, Nettie, morning, Gladys,' Grandfather's happy voice boomed behind me.

'Fred has the complete itinerary right up to boarding the Golden Eagle in Samarkand. All that's missing are disasters, shocks and surprises, and there will no doubt be plenty of those. Sorting them is my department, not Fred's. Come along, Nettie, the taxi is coming through the gate.' He opened the back door and ushered Nettie and myself into the back seat. 'Meet you at the airport.' Then he just disappeared.

We set off down the twisted roads and finally arrived at the main doors of the airport where Grandfather was waiting to pay the taxi driver and open our door. Nettie positively purred when he'd pair the fare and given the tip.

'Thank you, Chauncey. Pay you later.' He grunted and winked at me.

After that, it was so boring. Short run to London, transfer to British Airways and long overnight haul to Tehran. Grandfather once again there to meet us. Customs problems with British passports and cheese sandwiches. We were not in such good relations with Iran as we were with Persia, so we were regarded with deep suspicion and lots of gun belts. Passports were handed back with tweezers and twitching mustachios. Not a hint of 'Have a good stay, sir and madam'; just belligerent grunts.

Chapter Two

Grandfather hustled up a taxi and we were in the hotel in a short time where money paved the way from suspicion to smiles combined with the Chairman of the Board's PR perfect manners; 'Speaking their language always helps, dear boy.'

Nettie's room was the height of opulence, and ours was pretty good as well.

Dinner was a combination of Iranian and Western food ending with a hookah for Grandfather. He looked good, lying or semi-lying on piles of cushions. He started to cough and could not stop until he ended up almost collapsed and the pipework involved with his tip and hookah in pieces and water all over the cushions; 'prefer a cigar any day, dear boy. Nothing broken; just come to bits. I'll pay for the damage. I definitely prefer the American version of the hookah'.

Eventually, order was restored but we left the restaurant literally under a cloud.

The following day was on my list as sightseeing. Nettie wanted to see the national jewel collection housed in the vaults of the Central Bank. In the end, we forcibly had to pull her away. She was so absorbed by all the magnificence; she might even have attempted a robbery had we not. I reminded her how she pulled me out of places I wanted to see and she didn't. That was not diplomatic or even basically sensible. I lost.

'I shall come again, by myself, when we come back.' I knew only too well that she would, given half a chance, and the ensuing disaster would be a national incident in all the media.

Chapter Two

Chapter Three

The following day, we trooped out of the hotel to find our waiting transport - a sand-coloured 4x4 flatbed truck, as found on building sites, converted into a desert taxi by having two church pews fixed the length of the flatbed. These pews were prepared for use lined with plastic-covered cushions on the seat and the back, mean thin cushions with the odd carpet or rug thrown on to ensure greater comfort. A space had been kept behind the driver's cab for luggage; the final touch was a canopy of some red, thin material strung to four poles selected direct from a tree with knots and bark for authentic decoration. It was such a fragile structure, relying as it did on the material being tightly stretched between the poles. The slightest breeze combined with the speed of travel would see the whole edifice sailing across the Kavir Desert with gay abandon. 'Lovely colour for a dress!' was Nettie's comment.

Getting her into the vehicle was an exercise in itself.

The fat, amiable driver tried to persuade her to put one foot on the tailgate and he would push her up. She clung onto him with her vice-like grip and made it impossible for him to give her the necessary heave.

'I need someone to pull as well as push.'

The driver called to a couple of burly men obviously standing ready in the wings. This must happen on a regular basis, it was clear. They were big men and built up with perfectly toned muscles. Nettie was a feather-weight between them. With their back to the truck, they did the classic manoeuvre of one shoulder under each the armpit, other hands linked under her bottom, a united heave and she was up and staggering the length of the space between the pews. Grandfather, who had positioned himself in front of her, grabbed her hands and steered her to her place in a corner by the cab.

The driver just stood rubbing his arms where she'd gripped him.

Nettie immediately set about organising her corner to her liking. This included calling me to collect and bring to her the small green case with

Chapter Three

her pillows. This took time as it was buried under most of the rest of the luggage, but after a good clear out, I found it.

'Small green case, as requested.'

'Clear up the mess you've made; I cannot move here.' She then proceeded to put the small green case back where it had been.

'But Aunt Nettie, you've put the case you want back where it was. You haven't even opened it yet.'

'Don't be awkward, Fred. It was the blue case I asked for.'

I knew it was useless to argue. Nettie is never wrong, I let her get away with bullying me yet again; it was easier. Spineless is what Grandfather would call it, but then he's big and could squash her in an instant.

He, in the meantime, was dispensing large notes to the two strong men and the driver, issuing accompanying deep, approving growls and short Persian sentences.

'Fred,' Nettie called, 'do come and finish this clearing up. You've left such a mess,' so I dutifully jumped to it and was helped by the driver giving a final sweep to the floor. Nettie sat in the corner of the pew supported all around with cushions, her legs

Chapter Three

up on the seat, sunglasses and hat firmly in place. An extremely elegant Empress in her carriage, ready to make her triumphal appearance to delight the peasants. Totally unique and thank heavens for that.

I settled in the diagonally opposite corner to her Majesty, and Grandfather slapped the side of the truck as a signal to set off. 'I'm off to buy a suitable small stepladder for future loadings and off-loading. See you in Dom.'

Sitting in my corner as we drove through the streets of Tehran, I contemplated the suitability of this flatbed conversion. Each pew could probably take six or seven passengers, just looking at each other. It was hardly possible to see the buildings in the streets for bodies staring at you. Looking up to see the view of cliffs and mountains was blocked by the red canopy. As a sightseeing vehicle, it was a failure. As a taxi transporting people, it took a good load of paying punters, but not cultural ones. Travelling sideways was another problem. I wondered if Nettie had taken some of her seasickness pills, but I dared not ask, because if she hadn't, she would go into a panic even if she felt no effect. The driver was good; steady and sensible surrounded by chaotic traffic. Nettie appeared to have fallen asleep; her head was nodding with every bump in the road. People were begging or trying to sell things every time the traffic had to stop, which seemed to be every two minutes.

Eventually, we were out of the main town and on the way to Dom. My view was of the Kavir Desert and its salt lakes. Nettie's was over the Zagros Mountains behind me. In the distance, I could see Tehran in front of the Elburz Mountains leading to the Caspian Sea, a totally dramatic view full of contrasts and atmosphere. It seemed very foreign, and yet, to me, like where I was hatched. As I marvelled at the colours, a huge black bird took flight from the desert and soared up into the mountains behind us, swooping over the truck almost as if it was about to land. Instead, it deposited a huge splat on our red canopy, exactly over Nettie's head. She woke with a start.

'Is it cheese sandwich time?'

'Yes, I think it is.'

She pulled out a bag labelled CS (for cheese sandwiches) and another with a W (for water).

'There you are, Fred, I told you they'd come in handy.

Where's Chauncey? He's missing his lunch,' Said Nettie, the perfect hostess.

Chapter Three

'He's meeting us at Dom. He wants to buy a stepladder to get on and off our truck. The strong men were strictly in Tehran.'

'Nice thought, but the men were good. Very strong and efficient; no hesitation'.

'A portable stepladder will be better in the middle of the desert. It will be our own possession so we can always get you on or off anywhere.' She seemed to accept the logic but clearly regretted the strong men.

It was now getting vastly hotter; the sun was overhead and relentless; I just revelled in it, back to my origins. Nettie visibly wilted, fanning herself with a battery-driven hand fan that made an irritating squealing noise rather similar to a young piglet. She did not appear to hear it, but then she is deaf. I walked down to fill my tumbler out of the water bottle to find she had dropped off. The fan was held in her limp hands; I removed it and switched it off. Peace at last. There was no difference in the feelings of heat or the movement of air.

In other words, it was both useless and noisy. Come to think of it, I've met quite a lot of people like that - make a lot of noise but produce nothing. The sun bored vertically onto my head giving shadows and the world seemed to blank out. The desert had sparse growths of spikey shrubs looking like porcupines rather than vegetable growths. The smell was overwhelming. A mixture of sand, salt, vague manure from heated assorted animal's droppings. Everything was burnt to death, rather than rotted. I could see Dom (or Qom or Oom) in the distance, and, within minutes, we were driving down the main street to find Grandfather sitting at his ease at a table with a coffee pot and Persian goodies before him.

He stood up and signalled to our driver who promptly stopped alongside him. They had a conversation in Persian, at the end of which Grandfather picked up his newly acquired stepladder and he and the driver walked to the rear of the truck and set it up. It was a perfect fit, exactly the right size. Four sturdy steps, but no side support. Nettie, who was now awake, pointed this out in her usual commanding voice. Taking one hand each, the driver and Grandfather helped her, one step at a time, down to Terra Firma.

'There you are, Nettie, much more dignified.'

'I suppose you're right. Being pulled and pushed rather lowers the tone. Thank you very much.'

Chapter Three

'Come and have some coffee and goodies, ready for a sprint to Isfahan.' So, we all did and it was a jolly nice change from sitting in the truck.

'Well, off we go to Isfahan and a luxury hotel. Make a change for you from the dusty builder's truck.'

'With a giant bird's splat on it,' was my reply.

Grandfather had a funny look on his face. 'Precision bombing, wouldn't you say?'

'Very precise indeed; straight above Nettie's head.'

'Oh, you noticed that, did you? I was rather proud of that. Still there, adding to the shade of the canopy, yet taking the most accurate aim; not easy'.

'What sort of bird were you? I saw its size and blackness but had no clue as to what it was.'

'A black vulture; rare to these parts. Comes from Siberia. Likes it cold, but not the Siberian winters, that's more than a degree or two too far.'

Chapter Four

It was after dinner when conversation developed into plans for the furtherance of the journey. The ride from Dom had been, if anything, rather tedious. View to the left of the Kavir Desert, stretching to infinity, salt lakes and all. To the right, Zagros Mountains, soaring up to heaven, that is, if you could catch a glimpse from below the canopy without straining your neck. Isfahan was noisy, which surprised me. I had thought it would be regarded with respectful silence, but I suppose if you were born here, the usual familiarity would breed contempt.

It was not just native noises; it was tourist ones as well. European voices mingled with Middle Eastern to produce the polyglot Tower of Babel. Life was very much going on. Food smells mingling with the smell of the desert. Exotic perfumes from passing women in flowing robes and covered faces followed discretely behind their men meeting head-on with highly over-painted Western women with flowing and dyed hair dragging their men by the hand into shops selling gaudy or glowing metal trinkets and souvenirs. We had arrived at our hotel in the late afternoon, tired and full of sand, to be greeted with organised luxury and cool soft drinks. Nettie was lavished with attention and just lapped it up.

The route for our journey went across the Kavir Desert and into Turkmenistan, then into Uzbekistan to Samarkand. Approximately 1200 miles of distinctly hostile terrain, with no let-up anywhere.

'So, Aunt Nettie, it would be sensible to fly from Isfahan direct to Samarkand.' I heard my voice trying to sound forceful and positive, and failing completely. Nettie was not pleased, not at all. She glowered at me and her mouth formed a thin straight line. 'No, Fred, no.'

'Now look here, Nettie, we are both trying our best to see you have a good and comfortable journey. Yasser and his truck are no good for Turkmenistan; the terrain is too hostile and the roads can narrow to only five feet wide. The train seems to be once in a blue moon; it's either flying or camel. 1200 miles is far too much on a camel. From Bukhara to Samarkand is about 150 miles only, and I feel you could attempt that. If you fly to Bukhara from here, this solves the whole thing.'

Chapter Four

His voice was quiet and understanding, and I could see the beginnings of a meltdown in Nettie's anger towards me.

'Yes, Chauncey, I see your point. Fred has done exceedingly well but circumstances take over. Yasser is an excellent driver and his truck is all we could wish for, but if he refuses to go further, we must be prepared to change. I'm sorry, Fred, to have boiled up so angrily. Please forgive me.' I was so shocked by her apology that I couldn't think what to say.

'Fred accepts your apology, Nettie, and he's sorry that the options are limited. Let's go have a good time here in Isfahan, and go book a flight to Bukhara. Remember our deadline of October 17th for the Golden Eagle!'

'Good lad, Fred; all sorted.' I felt jubilant. Grandfather is such a remarkable and sensible dragon and so overwhelmingly kind.

I wandered through the hotel to the main entrance to breathe some air and hopefully lose some of the tension that always built up around Nettie. It was pleasant and cool out, and the sky was a mass of stars. A slight breeze brought a whiff of sweet-smelling flowers from the garden; I wandered down to the gate that opened into the desert. There was a noise like someone tapping or pecking on something hard and unyielding. I flew to the top of the wall and looked over. Tucked into the sand was an oval stone and the noise seemed to be coming from there. The stone bounced up and down in rhythm with the tapping. Suddenly, there was an extra loud tap, and the stone cracked showing a small nose that twitched.

A strong smell drifted up from the crack. Another heave and a wriggle and a complete pink head with pointed ears emerged from the hole with an accompanying squeal of obvious delight. The head moved from side to side, the nose smelling the air, the little eyes taking it all in. The stone cracked further and a rounded pink bottom emerged with a cute little tail all curled up neatly. I was thrilled to bits - a dragon hatching! I flew down from the top of the wall and helped pull the small being out of the shattered shell. I held out my hands and the little creature grabbed them and started to bounce up and down, feeling its feet and squealing happily. Its tail uncurled from its coil-of-rope shape and waved about; its right wing was still curled up, but the left one spread out very thoroughly. Something must be done with the right one, but the creature was so excitedly bouncing about. She was clearly a female; time for firmness. I lifted her up and carried her to a flat stone and sat her down. She clung to me and made life difficult, but I persisted and finally saw the problem. Pieces of shell had stuck in the wing. I carefully removed them and gently pulled the wing. It appeared to be quite normal, the bone structure sound and the fabric of the wing uninjured. I looked down at the newly hatched little dragon with love.

'Look, Milly, spread out both your wings like this.' I opened mine to help her understand. She did it! Both wings were in full working order with attendant squeals of delight as she rose from the ground.

'Jolly good, Milly,' came the familiar grandfatherly voice from behind me. 'Straightening that wing was the best thing you could have done. Getting the wings to work instantly is vital. If it's left, the whole becomes paralysed, usually for life. She's a grand little lady, full of life and fun.'

'Can we keep her?'

'Of course we can; in fact, we must. Dragon culture says that if we find a new hatchling, we must adopt and educate. We have no formal schools. We just pass our knowledge on so the new dragon carries on with all the background they need. If the teacher is not very good, you will not be either. I always say to ask questions and try to learn something new every day, good or bad. With a good background in basic magic, you'll survive for centuries.'

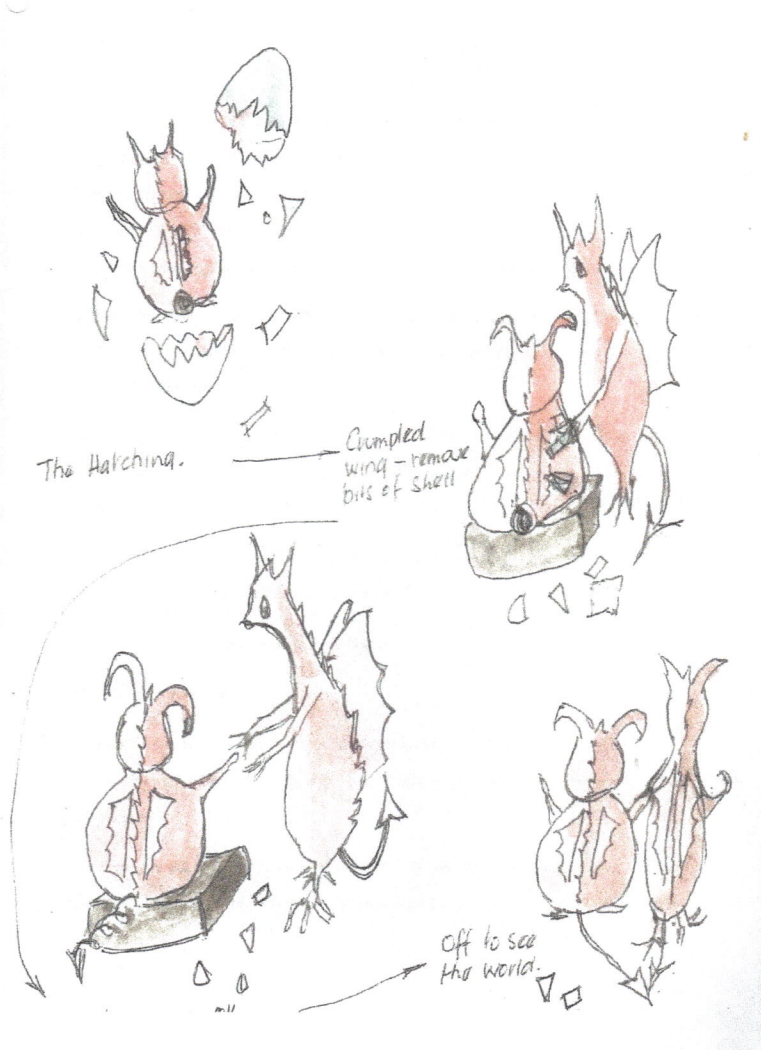

Chapter Four

Milly, in the meantime, had decided to use her wings again, and I suddenly realised she was sailing off into the desert. I whisked after her and turned her around, and we flew back to the hotel wall and Grandfather.

'Now, Milly, this will not do. You need flying lessons to teach you proper control, or all you will be able to do is fly forward and upwards.' Milly giggled and flung her arms around my middle.

'Fred, Fred, Fred!' she called and squeezed me tightly. 'Milly, Milly, Milly!' I said and squeezed her back. We both beamed at one another; life was good.

'We'd better go and introduce her to Aunt Nettie.'

This was not a good idea.

'Nettie will shrivel her to a cinder with one of her looks; she still does it to me.' The thought of Nettie was not a happy one. I held her hand firmly in mine and we followed Grandfather into the hotel.

'Oh, there you are at last. I've been waiting ages.' It was not her flirtatious voice. Nothing welcoming whatsoever. Milly tugged at my hand. I looked down at her sweet face now contorted with sheer naked terror. I squeezed her hand to give her some courage, but all it did was cause her to bury her head in my side and start to weep.

'Come, come, child, no snivelling. Nobody's going to hurt you.' Milly continued to cry and hid behind me.

'Stop that!' Nettie's voice reached its blast-off level.

'And you stop that bullying.' Grandfather's calm and kind voice broke through. 'Give her a chance; she's only been hatched an hour, and with a crumpled wing which Fred sorted out all by himself. She needs quiet kindness, not a full-blast dressing down.'

'Come along, Milly, I'll put you to bed.' I unpicked her from round my middle and lifted her into my arms. Her sobbing slowly ceased and she cuddled up to me whispering 'Fred, Fred, Fred' until she slowly fell asleep with a happy little sigh.

'There you are, Nettie, that's the way to do it.'

We took her upstairs to our room, definitely not Nettie's, and made a lovely cosy bed for her in a large armchair.

'Flying lessons tomorrow morning before it gets too hot. Good night, Milly darling. So glad to have found you.'

Grandfather fell asleep the minute his head touched the pillow. I drifted off slowly thinking about which lessons to start first.

But it was not to be. I was woken early by giggling squeals as Grandfather tried to get Milly off the ceiling.

'Milly dear, please let go of the light fitting and hang on to me.'

This was clearly far too big a sentence for her to comprehend so I whizzed up to their level, held onto Milly until she let go of the light fitting, then pulled her away and sailed down to the floor.

Grandfather looked an enormous bulk from underneath, particularly as his wings were open. He hovered like a great green edifice filling the space like a huge balloon that has broken its string. How one earth can I get him down? He did what he'd told Milly not to do and grabbed the light fitting, an elaborate chandelier, incorporating a fan as well as lights. Together with the green balloon, the whole lot came down with an almighty and very satisfying noise combined with a desperate wail. Milly and I rushed into a corner out of the way. Milly's eyes were popping out like stalks. The connection hole in the ceiling now produced a delightful shower of sparks falling down to the floor like a sparkly waterfall. Milly squealed her delight and ran into the room to catch the sparks as they fell.

'Grab her, Fred, before the whole place catches fire.'

I rushed to her and pulled her away out of danger. She did not like that and protested surprisingly violently, nearly knocking me over, just as a very loud knock combined with a bell sounded at the door. Grandfather was staggering about dazed, so I lifted Milly up and carried her with me to open the door. A group, consisting of the agitated manager, sub-managers and cleaners, was outside, all clearly full of concern. To greet them, the hole scattered more sparks. Grandfather held up a blade of the fan and said simply, 'It fell down!' and presented it to the main manager. That caused everyone to talk volubly and incoherently at once. Milly let out a piercing scream which nearly finished off my eardrums, but had the required effect of silencing the visitors with one complete cut-off.

It became clear that the manager was apologising for the fall of the chandelier, and was insisting on changing our rooms. Grandfather, who was clearly recovering, was accepting his apology with grace, but then, who would believe the truth?

We were conducted in a very orderly manner to a palatial room. Milly was given a lovely Uzbek cot, and I stood by the window watching the sun rise higher and higher and receiving our breakfast in the room with the multiple compliments of managers.

Chapter Four

'Well, Fred. Problem solved and without a word of a lie spoken.'

'Well, no single person would believe what really happened. Like sleeping dogs, let it all lie; unfair on the fixers.'

'But no international incident or very hefty compensation payment.'

Chapter Four

Chapter Five

Breakfast restored us all. Grandfather was back again in charge of the proceedings. 'Flying lessons, yes, but before that, we need a harness and an expanding lead. Down to the souk to find a good leatherworker. We can't start flying lessons until we are sure to have her under control! She's spirited and will want to fly away.' The leatherworker we eventually found seemed to get the requirements in a very short time, measuring round Milly both above and below the wings for a strap top and bottom, then another down between the wings to hold it all together. There was also a front panel in solid leather with the word Milly spelt out in twinkling silver bells. She was totally delighted and jumped up and down to make them work. She also saw a red bag with exquisite cutwork which she clearly wanted, so Grandfather agreed and the leather man was happy. We were happy, and Milly was up-in-the-clouds happy. When the bells rang, she squealed but it was a quieter squeal, more in keeping with the silver bells; quite charming. Grandfather was handed an extending lead and passed over bundles of notes which were accepted with great smiles. Everyone was happy, and we walked down the souk and out into the desert. The sun was gorgeous and hot and we were surrounded by people enjoying this charming little dragon.

There followed an hour of concentrated lessons, teaching her how to control her wings and make them do what she needed, but she was a remarkable pupil and got the grasp very quickly. Grandfather was even impressed enough to let go of his hold on the lead, and she hovered perfectly, untethered. We went for a short trip round a mound and back again in harmony and perfect control. Grandfather was impressed and praised her. She gurgled and said, 'Fred, Fred, Fred'. 'Yes, Milly, Fred helped, but you did the flying.'

Chapter Six

Grandfather organised some elevenses for us to recover from all our exercises. Milly was completely still up in the air, but a little quiet time helped her back to normal.

'I shall have to leave you for a few minutes to go to the airport and sort out a flight to Bukhara. I've no idea what day they fly there, but hopefully, it will be within our available time. Everything is gearing round the Golden Eagles on October 17th which is now six weeks away. We need several days to go by camel from Bukhara to Samarkand. Why Nettie can't agree about a straight flight from Isfahan to Samarkand, I just cannot imagine, but she's set on a camel with her cheese sandwiches. See you shortly.' Then he disappeared.

Being left with an excitable Milly was not my idea of a peaceful interlude, so I held on firmly to the lead and locked it at a short length. I began to think that Milly needed something under the harness to prevent her skin from being rubbed sore, so when Grandfather suddenly appeared back, I told him.

'Yes. Good idea; we'll buy her a dress to fit under. Nettie can help there.' At the name Nettie, Milly changed from a happy little dragon to a terrified one. She clung to me and would not let go. 'No Nettie, no Nettie, no Nettie.'

'Nettie is a fact of life and we must all deal with her. We are all here because she wanted to go to Isfahan and Samarkand. We found you here in Isfahan, and, according to dragon culture, we must now look after you. Nettie is good at dresses and will be able to set you up.' Grandfather's voice was kind and understanding to a terrified small being. Her eyes still looked scared to death, but his voice eased her fears somewhat. The mention of her name brought forth the actual dragon, long earrings and multiple necklaces included. Milly hid behind me, but Nettie winkled her out and fiercely stood before her.

Nettie weighed up the newly hatched dragon in front of her.

'I suggest a soft pale green and white, perfect for your very strong toned pink skin. Just straight down the front, no sleeves, and cut out at the back for each wing. No fastenings; the wings will keep it all in place. Slip it on over the head, no fuss, then Fred can fix the harness over it!' As she was talking, she marched us all through the souk until she found a dressmaker suitable to her liking.

Milly was measured up, down and round and a delightful fabric with a pattern of white flowers on soft green was pronounced the best choice.

Orders were given for two identical dresses. 'I wouldn't have thought of that,' Grandfather whispered to me. In very little time, the first dress was complete, so I removed the harness to allow it to be tried on. Milly was blissfully happy and jumped up and down and smoothed it over her plump stomach with clear pride. Her final act was to kiss Nettie on her cheek and beam at her lovingly. The price included matching knickers which were a complete mystery to Milly until Nettie showed her how to put them on. The whole party walked back to the hotel completely satisfied. All problems solved, Nettie looking happier than I have ever seen her.

Milly was, quite definitely, one of the family.

The flight to Bukhara was on the 18th of September, so we had two weeks to look around Isfahan, then plenty of time to go by camel from Bukhara to Samarkand.

In the afternoon, we walked around Isfahan marvelling at the tile and mosaic work. Milly went to bed exhausted, and when I called in to tuck her up, she had a pair of her new knickers on her head with her ears through the leg holes. A very sweet and charming sight!

Chapter Six

Chapter Seven

Having a whole fortnight in Isfahan made us all lazy. No need to rush anything. We walked all the squares, visited all the mosques and palaces, getting hopelessly muddled with the spelling. The big square Naghsh-e Jahan was impressive and unpronounceable and Sheikh Lotfollah mosque was equally so. By the end of the first week, we all had architectural indigestion. Arches, spires, domes, and minarets were transfixed on our eyelids when we eventually went to sleep. The sun burnt down, searingly hot, but no tile or mosaic faded in the heat. The elaborate patterns remained constant through high summer and bitter winter as they have for centuries, the intense blue of the sky captured forever.

Milly progressed by leaps and bounds. Her morning flying lessons became more intricate and exotic until she became almost a flying circus.

She and Nettie were getting on brilliantly well since the advent of the dresses and knickers. She had gone to see her with her knickers on her head, and was greeted with a cry of 'No, dear, those are not for your head', and promptly brought her some special white ones for sleeping in. Milly didn't really understand why there was so much fuss, but as Nettie was now her friend, she did as she was asked. Nettie, for her part, kept buying clothes, even going as far as a fur coat for winter. She looked like a teddy bear in this, and adored its soft fur, stroking it lovingly. In other words, Milly was thoroughly indulged to the point of being totally spoilt. Nettie took her for walks holding the end of the lead firmly so Milly could give her complete attention to all the dress shops without running or flying off.

Grandfather was delighted.

'Nettie has a project in hand. Keeps her off our backs, Fred.'

'Yes, but I miss it, being with Milly, sorting her out and giving her an education. There's only flying lessons left for us to be involved with, and she's such a good pupil. We're never going to be seeing her.'

'Don't fret; we have the mornings. Nettie's never up until midday.'

'I suppose so, but it was nice as it was.'

'It still is as it was, but we now have help with girly bits, and also, Nettie is off our backs all in one go. Let's have elevenses and enjoy life.' So, we did.

Chapter Eight

'So, dear boy, as Milly and Nettie are off shopping this morning, I think we should do a Dragon Flight to Bukhara and organise some camels and a driver (or whatever he's called) to take us to Samarkand, sorting out where we stay, how long it will take, and whether there are caravanserais on the road – a bit like motels -park your transport and have it attended to and fed, then sleep in a bed. Better for Nettie than bare earth in a tent. She will no doubt protest loudly that she is being deprived of the real experience and I'll have to explain that it is the full experience but in a later century, and not BC.'

'Very wise, Grandfather. Nettie snoring in a tent is strictly BC.'

We bade farewell to Milly and Nettie and next, we were touching ground in Bukhara and Grandfather started asking around for camels and a driver. He received the same name, Mustapha, so many times that he decided he must be rather the best, or most liberal with bribes over his network.

He proved to be an amiable chap wearing a long blue and white striped gown with a white turban. It was concluded that we needed four camels, one each and one for baggage. Milly would have to ride pillion or pommel; date, time, and meeting place were all established in a short time. Grandfather offered a small deposit, which caused Mustapha to fall about in delight. The extraordinary thing was that I could understand the conversation. It was obviously in some obscure dialect but I understood it, and, on one occasion, even joined in much to Grandfather's delight.

'You've finally triggered your language cells. You'll be able to talk to anyone now. We've always been able to do it, but some dragons never can. You'll pick up animals' language too. Talk shortly; great fun!'

I walked away hugging myself that I could understand language. This was a huge advantage which would make life infinitely easier.

When we arrived back in Isfahan, Nettie and Milly were back from their shopping, Milly jumping about with excitement showing us her new clothes for when we were to ride camels. They seemed a bit posh for the job, in my opinion, but then it was all Nettie's taste which could never be described as stark and

Chapter Eight

puritan. A good rollicking sand storm might change a few ideas on what was suitable. Deep turquoise velvet with silver trimmings was not. However, Milly adored it and stroked the velvet pile with real love, her fingers tracing the silver embroidery in real appreciation.

Nettie was not pleased that there was to be only one baggage camel.

'I have bought quite a few things like metal bowls and plates, and also an Uzbek cot for Milly.'

'Nettie, this is madness! We won't be able to take masses of extra luggage on the plane back to the UK, and anyway, Milly will outgrow a cot in the next few months. You must look ahead, and not just for today. The cot must stay here, not be carted halfway across the world.'

Oh dear; we were back to square one. Nettie versus the rest. The amnesty when Milly went over to Nettie's side had completely collapsed. Milly clearly was in a muddle and did not know which way to jump. She liked me and Grandfather but Nettie had produced all of these wonderful clothes, but she was still scary.

'We just have to keep steady, Fred, until she finds her feet. I just hope she comes down happy. We must just hang on and keep being and doing what we always have. Milly is bright; she'll see things straight in the end. She's still very, very young.'

Chapter Eight

The last few days before our flight to Bukhara were spent walking around Isfahan and flooding our brains with details of the incredible buildings. Founded by Shah Abbas, most of them were copied from those of Samarkand built more than 2000 years earlier. We in the Western world have nothing to compare it with. The tile and mosaic work is unique. Milly loved all the colours and patterns and stroked them where she could, making happy noises as she did.

Grandfather bought her a lovely one-piece romper suit, rain and windproof, secure at the neck, hands and ankles, so no sand or other nasties can get in. Also, a pair of boots to secure this further and a snug windproof hood. She would be all cosy and secure against any sandstorm, saving her beautiful velvet coat for special occasions. Milly was delighted and kissed Grandfather, much to his surprise. Nettie looked displeased and said so, but the practical use was explained to her, combined with the saving of the velvet for less hazardous times. Nettie huffed and puffed but wasn't convinced. Milly just kicked her little feet and cooed.

The day dawned for the flight to Bukhara, and we all turned up at the airport dressed for instant camel-riding. The flight was good, in a jet plane that was probably Russian, and we flew over Turkmenistan's rugged mountains, over the border into Uzbekistan and Bukhara Airport. Mustapha was waiting for us just outside the airport car park, his camels at ease sitting down, making grumbly noises and taking everything in.

Chapter Nine

Grandfather was very much in charge and had already turned us into humans for the flight. Mustapha treated him like God himself...it is amazing what a deposit will do! Milly held onto my hand securely. The idea of her going with Nettie did not occur, despite Nettie's controlling bossiness. I held on to her hand firmly, with my other one tight around her lead. Grandfather and I had spent a long time adjusting her harness straps to accommodate the romper suit, yet allowing for security and movement. The boots had caused bother, but they were finally properly fixed over the ankles. The trouble with Milly is that she can't, or won't, be still for a minute. We had a taxi to the airport as this was the only way to deal with Nettie's baggage, which was huge and complicated, even without the Uzbek cot. Grandfather threatened to leave her behind if she attempted to take it. As Nettie was still with us, she must have decided she needed us rather than the cot. I hoped it had been given to a true Uzbek baby, but history may give the answer.

In the meantime, Mustapha was leading us to the camels; they were four in number, one very posh and with long sweeping lashes round its huge eyes. It was obviously female and flirted coyly with Grandfather. He did not respond and just harrumphed, saying this must be Nettie's camel. Their combined breathing almost finished me off, and Milly tried to run me over; chaos!

Mustapha seemed a very nice man, eager to please and fussed around stacking Nettie's luggage on the sturdy camel he provided for the baggage. The only snag was the amount; Nettie kept two bags, one labelled CS for cheese sandwiches and the other W for water bottles. Mustapha's turban was badly fixed and bits kept falling down over his shoulders. His camels were immaculate, however. All leads were carefully stacked, rugs in place, saddles firm.

'Well, Nettie, it's time to get you on board. Mustapha and his son have nearly finished stowing the luggage; time for the passengers.'

Grandfather's hearty warm voice defied argument; I could see Nettie building up for a

blazing row, but her opponent stood firm.

Chapter Nine

'One leg up, hand on, then we'll give you a push for the other leg. Perfect, quite perfect.'

Mustapha came forward on the other side, and between the two of them, she surprisingly slid into place.

'My back needs support.' Mustapha produced a backrest, adjusted it to Nettie and the camel, then sorted all the straps on both sides.

'Get out of that!' Grandfather whispered in my ear followed by an agreeable harrumph. Nettie, realising it was over, gave up and accepted her fate. She looked uncomfortable now on a still camel, but what would happen when it moved? Watch this space!

'Milly; I must have Milly with me.'

'No, Nettie, Milly goes with Fred. He is her guardian, not you. We call you in for things we cannot do, like her dresses, but you are not her guardian.' On these words, Milly jumped behind me and clung to my hand. I squeezed it tight and smiled down at her and she relaxed and smiled back. I was pleased too because Grandfather had officially given me status as her guardian. Nettie was cross, very cross, and protested by banging both her feet into the camel's neck. The camel responded thinking it was being given instructions to move, and carefully began

to stand up, one leg at a time. Nettie, unprepared for these movements, swung forwards and sideways alarmingly, but her strappings and backrest held firm, and although her centre of gravity came over that of the camel, she did not fall off. Mustapha went to calm both camel and rider and led them away from our group and out of shouting distance.

So, Nettie sat on her camel fuming, too far away even to shout. Grandfather indicated that it was now our turn to mount, and led me and Milly to our smaller beast. The poor thing looked very apprehensive after seeing the performance with Nettie. Milly and I flew up together, linked by the lead. I had a good saddle in front of the hump, and Milly had a special small one lined with cushions in front of me. We settled in and Grandfather fastened our straps. Milly kicked her little feet with pleasure to the extent that I had to restrain her in case the camel got the same wrong idea as Nettie's had.

Now it was Grandfather's turn. We had all reverted to dragons for the journey, and consequently, were rather untidy with tails and wings to accommodate. Grandfather couldn't accommodate, and his tail was wound round the body of the camel alarmingly. The poor beast had the addition of his weight to deal with and was not happy. Grandfather clung on, unstrapped, for a minute or two, and then slowly subsided off to the right. There were bellows and shouts, and Mustapha came running, but too late. Grandfather hit the ground with the poor animal underneath and around him. It was a picture to see, all legs, tails and terrified large eyes. Grandfather managed to slide away sideways and resume a semi-standing position. Mustapha comforted poor thrashing Yassa until he finally calmed down and managed to ease into a position where he could stand. Milly was delighted with the entire incident and cheered him on. Our camel went up to the struggling Yassa and gave him a brotherly nudge which helped him gain his feet. A few tugs of the lead straps and he was up, shaking his head.

'I shall fly the rest of the journey,' the familiar voice abounded.

'You ok, Fred?' 'Yes, we're ok.' Milly squealed in unison.

'Are all our party plus luggage in order?' We nodded. 'Then let us begin.'

Chapter Nine

Chapter Ten

With Mustapha leading the empty camel Yassa, we set off through Bukhara. Nettie, on the flirtatious Clem, was second, and we were third, with Alpha, the baggage beast, behind us. Grandfather disappeared completely but I caught the odd glimpse of him between decorated high towers. The way to Samarkand was through a fruitful (literally) area alongside the River Zarefshan. The greenery of the trees and sown land extends both sides of the river, and beyond these fields is a pasture for flocks. Every town and settlement has a fortress. It is said to be the most fruitful of all the countries of Allah. In every home are gardens, cisterns, and flowing water. Wild desert. Very much not the sort of journey that Nettie hankered after. It was, in fact, a perfect country to travel through, except for the camels which moved in such a wobbly way that it made you dizzy.

Nettie complained loudly.

'Where is Chauncey? I must talk to him now, this minute. This countryside is very pleasant but no good for camels. We need desert and wild country, not a market garden.'

'This is all there is around here. Samarkand is in a very fruitful place; be thankful. The camels have an easy time in this terrain. Water in abundance, happy people, well-fed.'

'My camel wobbles too much; it makes me feel ill.'

'I told you before we left England that camels make you seasick, but you wouldn't listen. We've tried our best to organise this trip for you, but we didn't mince words. Camels wobble and riders with them, hence sea sickness.'

'When I travel, I need to stay quiet in a cabin, not be thrown about on a lumpy beast. It hasn't even a smooth back to sit on. It's all lumps and knobbly bits and is uncomfortable even standing still. Then it moves and is infinitely worse. Get me a car! We could be there in four hours. 177 miles. I want a car!'

'For heaven's sake, have a few cheese sandwiches on the back of a camel, then you've completed the instructions you gave us and I'll get you a car.' The exasperation in Grandfather's voice could be cut with

Chapter Ten

a knife. Milly and I kept quiet and just waited. The next two minutes would either see the problem solved or the whole world blown up. Nettie, in her own bubble, began to open her cheese sandwich boxes, completely ignoring the chaos she had unleashed.

'Fly up, Fred, and collect your favourite.' I tied Milly's lead to my saddle and flew across to the extended offering. 'And one for Milly, too.' Mustapha was clearly going quite mad with this crazy woman and appealed to Grandfather as to his future.

'I must go to Samarkand with all my camels because I have another journey booked from there. I must carry on, Your Excellency.'

'Of course you must, and the rest of us will come with you. Only Madam will be missing.'

We ate our sandwiches and drank our water in total silence, only broken by the sound of a 4x4 driving towards us. The vehicle stopped alongside us, and Grandfather indicated a lay-by a little further on, so Mustapha led Clem and her passenger to meet the car. Clem lowered herself gently to the sitting position and the two men helped Nettie disembark. As she slid to the ground, they each took an elbow and walked her across to the car. Mustapha opened the back door and Grandfather handed her in.

'Here's some money, Nettie, for the car and three nights in the hotel. We should be there then and our expedition will continue. Goodbye Nettie, see you in a few days. Do not buy anything, as we cannot take more baggage. I've put your overnight case in the car with you; the rest will come with us.' The door shut with a resounding clunk. There was a wonderful feeling of relief, and we all waved as the car drew away in the direction of Samarkand.

Chapter Eleven

The next few hours were extremely pleasant. Camels in order as before, but two empties this time. The sun was hot, but the abundant trees gave dappled shadows on the road. The landscape was beautiful, every inch tended. No sand or scrubbiness at all. The camels obviously enjoyed this and ambled gently along with no serious wobbling. Mustapha's turban was so loose, it was almost off his head, so I suggested we stop for him to have the few minutes it would take to re-tie. He ended with a perfect turban looking very smart and organised. Milly wanted to fly, and I saw no problems, and let her go to the longest length of her lead. She flew between the trees utterly happy, came back, settled down and went to sleep. Grandfather walked with us, now and again flying a few miles; he was happy too.

Gradually, the light began to fade and Grandfather talked to Mustapha who said he was aiming for a caravanserai around the next corner, and there it was; a fortress on the hillside. We were heartily welcomed and fed, and our camels equally cared for in very good stables. Mustapha was happy. It was a beautiful night, deep blue sky studded with stars, soft scents drifting on the breeze; a thoroughly good place. Milly woke me at dawn, insisting on a flying lesson.

We flew together down the road, then I guided her up above the trees over the pasture area. Milly loved this pure freedom. She suddenly squealed and pointed to a hill in the middle distance. There were ten or twelve men on horses, and the men were looking in our direction with binoculars or long spyglasses. The men all had matching pale blue turbans. I did not like this, as the whole effect was military, including the horses.

'This is not good, Milly. We need to talk to Grandfather.' I turned her around and we flew back to the fortress. Grandfather was delighted to see us because he thought we had been kidnapped. I described the group of men and he was all ears.

'Mustapha warned me yesterday of a gang of bandits milling round. I must talk to him immediately. This is the last thing we need. Milly found them, you say? Sharp eyes, Milly.' We went to the stables, and as I passed a doorway, I saw Mustapha talking to a man in a pale blue turban. This was not good. If Mustapha was in with the gang, what hope had we?

'You and Milly stay here, and I'll get to the bottom of this. We are far from a large and wealthy caravan; we're not worth attacking…no large spoils.'

Grandfather butted into his conversation with the blue turban. Mustapha became red in the face and agitated; blue turban left the stables with an obvious see-you-later sort of dismissal.

Grandfather looked fiercely at Mustapha.

'So, this is the way you make your money. Leading your clients into the gang's trap, at the same time building up your reputation as an honest and reliable driver of good camels.'

'But, Excellency, I was only telling him that you were a small party with no great riches. One baby, one small boy, and yourself. Not worth their effort.'

'But why were they looking in our direction with spyglasses?'

'Because a large caravan is following yours. I was telling him when you joined in.'

'You are a rogue in league with bandits. You are good with your camels. Stick to them and don't get involved with banditry.' Mustapha hung his head. 'His Excellency does not know how well bandits pay for information.' He looked at Grandfather's stern face and decided to avoid speaking.

'We will leave in an hour; be ready.'

'Yes, Excellency, one hour.' We parted company.

'Are we safe now, Grandfather?'

'Perhaps, but not for the long haul. Mustapha is clearly onto a good thing and has access to masses of information.'

So, within the hour we set off. Two empty camels, one baggage, and one camel with two passengers. Lovely day, hot but not too much so, camels amiable. Milly was very bright and lovely after her morning's fly. I just felt bewildered and very unhappy about the prospect of being attacked. Grandfather assured me that he could cope with any eventuality. I wanted to believe him but somehow his collective disasters kept coming to mind. This was not to the standard of the first one, but adequate, according to Mustapha.

The light had faded from the sky and a gentle darkness took over. Milly fell asleep cuddled up to me, when there was a noise like the rush of water down a hill, and I looked up to see blue turbans on strong horses belting towards us. It was extremely alarming. Grandfather, who was walking beside my camel, tugged the reins and looked into my face.

'Hang on; look after Milly and don't worry; I'll deal with all of this.'

The line of horses was so near you could smell their breath and I was scared witless. Grandfather let out a great flame from his mouth which terrified the horses into stopping dead in their tracks and their riders could not control them. There was another burst of flames and the whole gang were engulfed in a dense fog. There was total silence for a couple of minutes, then the slight breeze caused by movement blew away the fog, leaving absolutely nothing. No blue turbans, no curved cutlasses, no horses; just nothing. Not even a footprint. Grandfather harrumphed at least three times. 'Haven't done that for years but the system still works. We'll not see anything of them ever again. Mustapha's lost his income. He'll have to be just an official camel driver and not gather information for the Middle Eastern Mafia.'

Chapter Twelve

With no threats now looming, we made our way to the accommodation for the night.

First things first, the camels had stone-built stables with mangers and water troughs. We had tents, very basic ones, with holes to let in hot and cold draughts depending on the circumstances. Wonderfully, they provided a sweet little Uzbek cot for our lively baby. She squealed and squealed then rolled and humped until she had a good thing going then rocked the night away. Dawn broke at least an hour before she did; she now lay dead to the world. The heat of the sun warmed the tent, but nothing could rouse her. I even tried the two words 'flying lessons' loudly in her ear, but no response. Our sweet little baby did not want to join our world. We ended up dressing her in her romper suit completely unconscious.

'At least she doesn't wriggle or squeal. Quite peaceful for once…enjoy!' So, we did. We were brought a hearty breakfast to set us on the road and Milly was strapped into her saddle with both eyes firmly shut.

It was a really good day, peaceful and happy, but all the time I was nagged by a thought.

'Grandfather, I am bothered. This journey was organised for Nettie and she's now opted out. I think we should persuade her to get back on a camel at the gates of Registan Square then take her photograph, and have her go on for about ten feet before she's allowed off. It seems only right, don't you think?'

'Perfect, Fred. I'll get Mustapha to go meet her and we will all go through the gate together. Mission complete!'

Grandfather and Mustapha had a conference and I felt better. These trips are Nettie's, after all. So, the three of us spent our last night in a caravanserai, a reasonably comfortable one this time, under a solid roof and on beds, not on the ground. Milly was quiet with no squeal, no fear of bandit raiders.

'Where did they go, Grandfather? How did they just disappear like that?'

'Some questions are best not asked. I haven't the faintest idea - the spell I was taught just removes only. They may be roaming about in another continent, or have been turned to dust of the desert. Whatever,

Chapter Twelve

they won't bother us. Another two or three weeks, we shall all be on another continent, so we won't get to find out. Not a very satisfactory answer to your question, but the best I can do'.

'Well, you always tell me to ask questions, so I do. Let's forget the whole thing and enjoy our last night with the camels. Next stop, London Zoo, bad breath and seasick rides.'.

The following morning, he informed us that he'd been to see Nettie in her hotel and put forth my proposal about coming into Samarkand through the gate, four or five steps, then a record by photograph for the archive. She had been delighted with the thought and was looking forward to it all. Mustapha would come with us and he would arrange for Clemestra to be sitting waiting for her to mount. Our journey did not seem long today; the end was in sight!

All the arrangements went well. Nettie had dressed herself up to have her photograph taken so the journey finished on a high. Nettie was extremely complimentary to me for thinking of asking her to join in. She really was becoming quite civilised.

Mustapha had gathered his camels together to set off on his new commission, nobody saying a single word about his association with the bandits. A perfect journey's end.

Chapter Thirteen

Samarkand is old. Very, very old. One of the oldest continually inhabited cities in Central Asia. Some theories propose it was founded between the 8th and 7th centuries BC, prospering from its position on the Silk Road between China and the Mediterranean. It was conquered by Alexander the Great in 329 BC. He respected it, unlike Genghis Khan who devastated it in 1220 AD.

The Turco-Mongol leader, Timor, imported artisans to repair it and make it his capital. Marco Polo reported it depleted but recovering. Timor, or Tamerlane as he was known, took a personal interest in all construction. Being lame, he was carried around all sites in a litter. The Bibi Khanum Mosque cracked and had to be rebuilt, the moral being don't build in a hurry, particularly if you want centuries of use.

The old town is exotically beautiful to Western eyes and takes your breath away, but the modern city around it, including the Soviet flat blocks, swamps it. A perfect rare jewel set in an anthill.

Inhabitants are polyglot and of all colours and creeds, mixed nowadays with tourists from all over the world. Amazingly, it all survives, and Tamerlane's artists work remains as fresh as when first built. The water from the river feeds the countryside which is fruitful in the extreme. All houses have cisterns and running water, fountains and ponds. There is grazing for animals and plenty of trees; paradise in a barren land.

Apologies for giving a lecture about the city, but it cannot be described in a few short words. A place unique in the world, utterly beautiful and still alive after sackings and rebuildings. The architecture takes all breath away and you can soak up its beauty and have your soul restored. The history engulfs you and you can feel you are part of Tamerlane's world.

We walked round the place, its colleges, squares and mosques, in our own time. You must go there one day and see for yourself.

In what seemed like no time, it was October 17th and we were at the station waiting for the Golden Eagle to appear. We had two suites, one for Nettie and one for the rest, and we settled in for the long ride to Tehran. Russian passengers spent most of their time in the various bars and became increasingly rowdy over the ensuing days. Food was typical; East Asian combined with not very typical Western. Milly was noisy and frustrated at not being able to fly. One morning, she woke us up with great squeals, her little arms pointing to the windows trying to describe what she'd seen. It was snow! The first in her life. The engine was just slowing down to enter Bukhara, where we were due a long stop. Milly dashed out into this pretty white stuff falling all around her. She delighted in the snowflakes with all their myriad shapes, and almost cried when they turned to water drops on her clothes. Grandfather made snowballs and threw them, but on the whole, there was very little to play with, just a sprinkling, but it was fun while it lasted.

Nettie, of course, missed the whole lot; she never woke up in time.

'Mornings are not my time; you know that, Chauncey.' Chauncey did. Snow was always there in the background adding a feather eiderdown to the mountains but we were restricted to occasional flurries only for the afternoon.

Our suites were luxurious. Comfortable beds, dining table and chairs, dressing table, hanging wardrobes and drawers. We had to ask for a cot for

Chapter Thirteen

Milly as there were no armchairs to make her bed on. The dining room was opulent with a feeling of the time of the Czars. There was basic roof lighting with strip lights behind the cornice and wall lights shaded with pleated peach fixed to ornamental brackets on the walls.

The curtains were lined with silk and curved and quilted pelmets hung over the windows on both sides of the carriage. Comfortable chairs with rounded backs sat at tables on both sides of the carriage. The tablecloths and other linen were all white. The whole was more like a Parisian restaurant rather than a train.

The bars varied, with hints of 1930's cinema with square deep armchairs down the length of both window walls; they looked as if they should be comfortable, but were definitely not. The bars looked well-used as if the point of the journey was to spend the entire time there drinking.

Bathrooms were small but adequate with shower and basin in addition to basin and WC. The shower was a bit small for Grandfather and he managed to get himself stuck.

'Must eat a bit less tonight, there's more of me than there should be.'

Altogether, it was a good train, probably Russian rolling stock with coach-fitters told to fulfil their wildest dreams of luxurious life. It wasn't busy, particularly for the last train, but then the price was sky-high. We all enjoyed it in our separate ways.

Milly went totally wild, running up and down the corridors and the service-ways down the centre of the dining cars. She threatened to cause complete grief if a member of staff was carrying a tray, so we put her in her harness and kept her firmly in check with the lead. If she dodged the lead, the bells gave warning of her approach in time to devise a counter-coup. The staff all round were magnificent. No extra job was too much, no thoughtful task undone, all with a smile, and clear delight in Milly's presence. They adored her, and she them. The sound of the tinkling bells in the next carriage brought out smiles on whatever part of the train; she made it a jolly as well as luxurious way to travel. She talked all the time, utter gibberish in any language, but there were so many different languages aboard, nobody seemed to understand anyone else anyway. Just riotous chaos to the accompaniment of silver bells. Milly was definitely a star without question.

'We've picked a right one here, dear boy. Little did you know, when you saw her hatch, what life we would be in for.'

Chapter Thirteen

'I only did my duty as a dragon. You taught me that. She just adds to life, makes it worth living. Come along, Milly, let's go have our lunch.'

The train was not continuously moving. It stopped at various wonderful places where coaches took parties round outstanding ancient towns, palaces and mosques. Nettie refused to budge, so we three flew off on our own. In the Iranian border town of Sarakhs, there was compulsory evacuation, so we had to disembark, and go over the border in coaches for passport control, no doubt making certain no unwanted person came into the country. We English humans were let through reluctantly and were profoundly glad we were allowed to re-board.

Chapter Thirteen

No further tourist visits for us - Tehran and off home, no arguments.

Back at the debriefing, I finally managed to get in the question that had bothered me.

'Grandfather, how did you manage to produce a British passport for Milly? None of us know who her parents are and she was born in Isfahan in Iran, of all places.'

'Yes, dear boy, a good question…harrumph… I flew back home in the night when you were all asleep and registered her. Nobody raised an eyebrow, nobody asked unanswerable questions. Just father deceased, mother died at birth, guardian at birth Frederick Nogard. Place of birth Isfahan, Iran. They looked a bit non-plussed at that because it seems they thought it was the name of a house, but they accepted everything and hoped we all had a good journey home. End of story. No fibs or exaggerations. The whole truth would be unbelievable. Hatched under a hotel wall. No box to tick for that. She now holds a British passport and good luck to her. Her address is Jane's house. I paid the money and did a dragon drive back to the Golden Eagle. No sweat.'

There was absolutely nothing I could say, so I kept quiet.

Nettie came in at that point, full of herself, saying how she would like a trip up the Nile next year.

The silence that statement produced was broken by Grandfather.

'We all thought that this was your last trip before being strung on wires in the British Museum.'

'Oh, no! I have been invigorated by seeing Samarkand; I need a look at Egypt before the end.'

'We promise nothing, Nettie. It depends on what happens next year. We have got Milly to consider now. We will talk later.'

His voice tailed off and I thought of Milly stuck on top of a pyramid or lost in a tomb.

My enthusiasm faded but Nettie's did not.

Chapter Fourteen

Grandfather came into the room as I was researching ancient Egypt. 'Have a look at the extract from The Times. Interesting, to put it mildly.' I took it from him and placed the short article in a good light.

'Remarkable find now in the British Museum.'

An archaeology student walking along the beach on the Jurassic Coast in Dorset was halted by the sight of a new crack in the cliff above him. Rocks had fallen away revealing a widening of an existing crack. Being curious at all times, he climbed up and wriggled his way into the cliff. After about two yards of narrow tunnel, it opened out into a large cave, full of daylight from a large ragged hole in the domed roof. Below the hole on the cave floor was a skeleton, a small one of a human female with delicate bones and a finely chiselled skull. There was no trace of flesh, but some pieces of fabric. The extraordinary thing was that the skeleton was adorned with a mass of jewellery. Earrings on the ground but no ears to hold them. Multiple necklaces still around the neck bones. The student took many photographs then worked his way back out of the cave and rang a colleague who worked at the British Museum. The colleague alerted his seniors who dropped their plans and came post-haste to see this unique find.

It took a very long time to remove the skeleton. This involved the construction of a tower crane to raise the padded coffin to the only exit, the hole in the roof, skilled builders to do the hauling, and security for the whole, but particularly for the jewellery. There was a great cheer when her remains finally cleared the surroundings to the hole and the procession began down the road at the base of the hill. As she was being loaded into the waiting van, there was a deep rumble and crash followed by a huge cloud of asphyxiating stone dust as the top of the hill imploded into the cave. The silence that ensued was profound, with an aftermath of great peace.

The British Museum has issued the following statement:

"We have received a skeleton of a small human being, most likely female, whose bones indicate origins from the Cretaceous and Tertiary eras. This particular skeleton is at least 2000 years old, but appears to have died within the last two years. She is a total enigma and requires a great deal of further investigation before any conclusion can be given. With origins in the age of birds and reptiles, long before Homo sapiens developed, she has evolved on a different path from those related to apes. She could be a separate development not thought of before, or just a throwback to the Cretaceous period. Further evidence must be sought. She has the vestiges of wings, obviously atrophied, but part of her bone structure. There is evidence of a tail, surgically removed using modern equipment and techniques. She shows no evidence of manual labour. Her hands and feet have three digits each, no problem when you wear shoes, but hands would show. Her jewellery is valued in the millions. Several items are from the 20th century, but others are obscure and need investigation. Something to give considerable thought. She will not be on display until further knowledge is obtained."

'Well, dear boy, what is your opinion of all that?'

'Basically, I think I can forget any further research on Egypt. It must be Nettie; it must be.'

'That's my opinion as well. She said she was going to Peru to see Oswald. I last saw her months ago. I cannot understand this reluctance to divulge anything. Is she important historically or not? If she is, so I must be. We hatched together, after all.'

'Maybe apes are one source for humans and we are another. Trust Nettie to cause the very proper fuss and involve everyone. It just has to be Nettie; it's just her style. Always with panache.'

'Yes, and buckets of jewellery thrown in. A time to keep quiet and leave things to others.'

'Even though I'm convinced it is Nettie, half of me is sure she will just turn up one day, all as before, awkward and bossy as she always was, but with just as much elegance and style. She can't have gone forever. She'll put human scientists into a spin and turn history inside out, then appear as if nothing has happened.'

'Wait and see, Fred, you might be right.'

'What do I do about the Nile?'

'Just let it flow, and catch up later.

In the meantime, let's have elevenses.'

So, we did.

Chapter Fourteen

Milton Keynes UK
Ingram Content Group UK Ltd.
UKHW051029030124
435356UK00010B/178